PJMASKS
Time to Be a Hero

Based on the screenplay
"Blame It on the Train, Owlette"

Ready-to-Read

Simon Spotlight
New York London Toronto Sydney New Delhi

Connor, Amaya, and Greg
are at the fair.
"I want to ride the train!"
Amaya says.
But where is it?

The train is gone!

The PJ Masks can find it!

Greg becomes Gekko!

Connor becomes Catboy!

Amaya becomes Owlette!

They are the PJ Masks!

Owlette really wants
to ride the train.

She is in a rush
to find it.

Owlette jumps into
the Cat-Car.
"Come on!" she says.

She uses her Owl Eyes

to see far away.

Owlette sees the train!

Romeo is driving it!

Romeo is using the train to chase his lab. His lab is zooming around the city by itself. He wants to catch it.

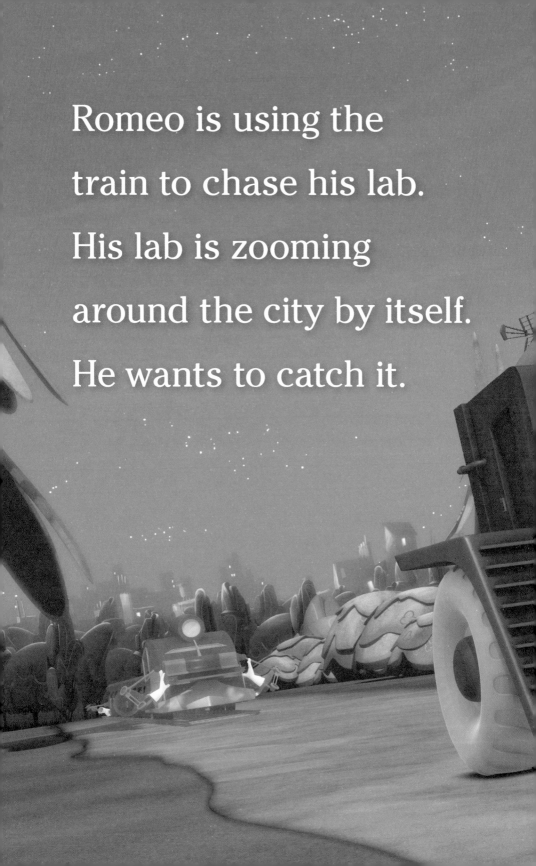

The PJ Masks jump

onto the train!

Owlette rushes ahead

to stop Romeo.

"Wait for us!" Gekko
and Catboy say.
Romeo catches Owlette!

Gekko and Catboy

help her escape.

"I am sorry," Owlette says. "I should have listened and not rushed. It is time to be a hero!"

Owlette has a plan.
The PJ Masks will
work together.

Catboy gathers
some branches.

He throws them to Owlette.

Gekko climbs onto the train.

Owlette throws the
branches to Gekko.
He jams the train tracks
with them!

The train is out of control.

Gekko is very strong.

He stops the train.

The train cars swing around the lab and trap it.

Romeo leaves the train.
He is so happy to have
his lab back.

PJ Masks all shout hooray!

Because in the night,

we saved the day!

The PJ Masks return
the train to the fair.
The day is saved!

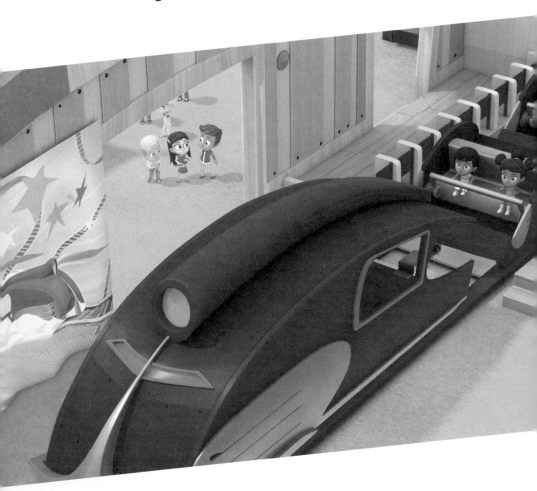

PJ Masks Save the Library!

Based on the episode
"Owlette and the Flash Flip Trip"

Ready-to-Read

Simon Spotlight
New York   London   Toronto   Sydney   New Delhi

Amaya is excited to read her Flossy Flash superhero book.

Oh no! Someone erased all the stories!
The books just have pictures of Romeo inside!

This looks like a job
for the PJ Masks!

Greg becomes Gekko!

Connor becomes Catboy!

Amaya becomes Owlette!

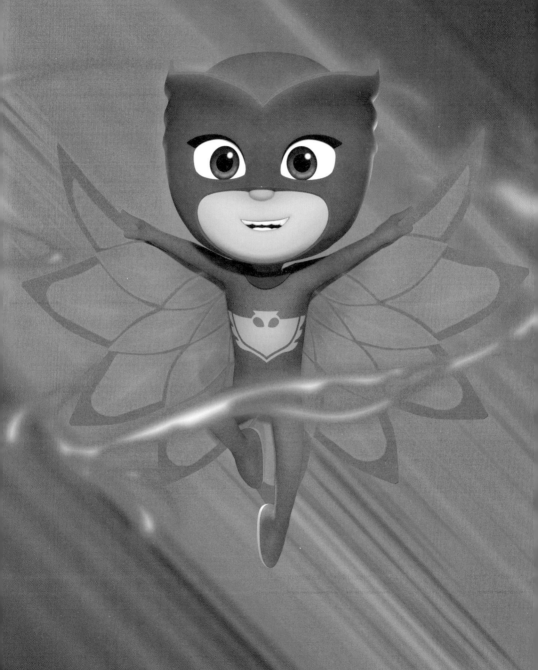

They are the

PJ Masks!

Owlette is reading
her Flossy Flash book.

She wants to be
like Flossy Flash.

In the Cat-Car,
Catboy asks Owlette
to use her Owl Eyes
to find Romeo.

Owlette wants powers
like Flossy Flash instead.

Catboy hears Romeo
with his Super Cat Ears.

Oh no! Romeo ruined more books and is escaping!

"Where will Romeo
go next?" Catboy asks.

"To the library!"

Gekko shouts.

"We have to stop him!"

The heroes make a plan.
Gekko climbs high with
his Super Lizard Grip.

He asks Owlette to look
for Romeo with her
Owl Eyes.

Instead, she pretends to
be Flossy Flash!

She forgets to look

for Romeo!

"Robot!" Owlette cries
when she sees Romeo and
his robot.

Owlette is too late.

Romeo ties up

Gekko and Catboy!

"I will save you with
my Flossy Flash Flip!"
Owlette says.

Owlette trips and falls.
Romeo laughs and steals
all the library books!

"I should have used
my owl powers,"
Owlette says.

"Time to be a hero!"
she says. She sets
Catboy and Gekko free.

She uses her Owl Eyes
and Super Owl Wings
to look for Romeo.

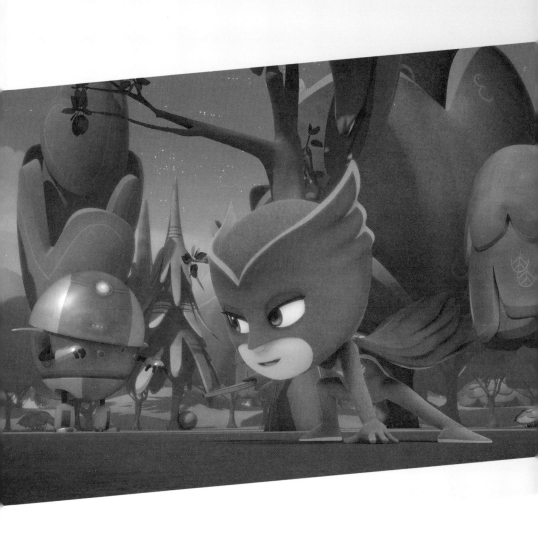

She sees Romeo.

"I still have my book!"

she shouts.

Romeo and his robot
chase her!
Catboy and Gekko
tie up the robot!

The PJ Masks fix all

the books.

They save the library!

Super Cat Speed!

Based on the screenplay
"Catboy's Great Gig"

Ready-to-Read

Simon Spotlight
New York   London   Toronto   Sydney   New Delhi

The school concert
is tomorrow.

But where are

the instruments?

This is a job

for the PJ Masks!

Amaya becomes Owlette!

Greg becomes Gekko!

Connor becomes Catboy!

They are the PJ Masks!

Catboy is scared.

He does not want

to play in the concert.

What if he messes up?

The PJ Masks hear

a harsh noise.

It is Night Ninja!

Night Ninja is singing.

The Ninjalinos have
the missing instruments.

Catboy will use his
Super Cat Leap
to trap the Ninjalinos
with a net.

But he is too afraid.

It does not work.

"If we cannot get the instruments back, I guess the concert is off," says Owlette.

Catboy does not like
to see his friend sad.

Catboy uses Super Cat Speed!

He speeds around
the Ninjalinos.

He takes back one of the instruments.

It is a recorder.

Catboy will need to
play the recorder.
Everyone is watching,
but Catboy must be brave.

Catboy plays the recorder.

He is really good!

The Ninjalinos like
playing with Catboy
more than Night Ninja.

They leave Night Ninja!

Then Owlette and Gekko

trap Night Ninja in a drum.

The Ninjalinos give
the instruments back.
"I will get you for this!"
Night Ninja says.

PJ Masks all shout hooray!

Because in the night,

we saved the day!

Catboy learned that
it is okay to be afraid,
but always do your best!

Hero School

Based on the episode
"Looking After Gekko"

Ready-to-Read

Simon Spotlight
New York   London   Toronto   Sydney   New Delhi

Greg is excited to take a
book home from school.

Greg reaches for a book.

It is too high.

Greg falls.

Connor and Amaya get
the book for Greg.
They walk to the
school bus.

Oh no! The school bus
is missing!
This looks like a job for
the PJ Masks!

Amaya becomes Owlette!

Greg becomes

Gekko!

Connor becomes
Catboy!

They are the PJ Masks!

Gekko wants to drive.

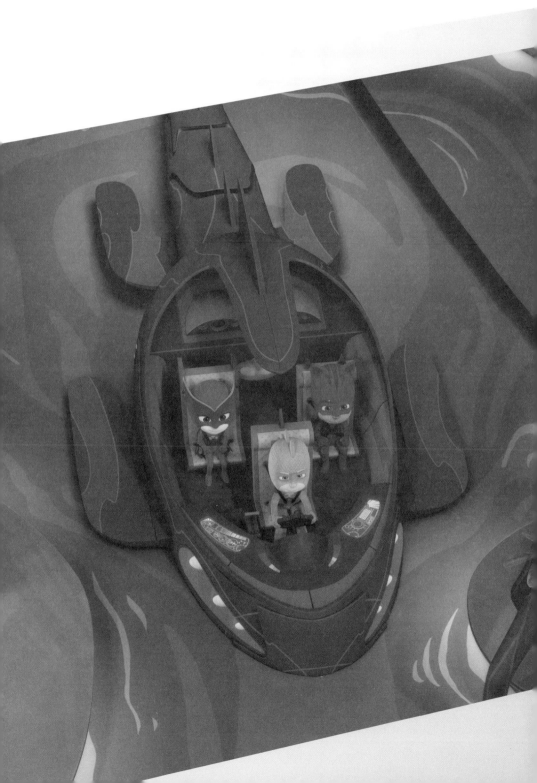

The PJ Masks see the
school bus! They chase it.

The Gekko-Mobile
is too slow.

The bus gets away.

"Cat Ears!" says Catboy.

"Owl Eyes!" says Owlette.

They find the bus
using their powers.

The bus is in the town square! Gekko wants to be the hero.

Gekko drives to
the town square.
Night Ninja has the bus!

The Ninjalinos are
painting the bus blue.
"Give back the bus,"
Gekko says.

"No! The bus will be
my super-car!"
Night Ninja says.

Night Ninja throws
Sticky-Splats.

Gekko is in trouble!

Owlette and Catboy arrive.
"We will help, Gekko!"
they say.

Gekko does not want help.

Night Ninja throws
Sticky-Splats at Catboy.

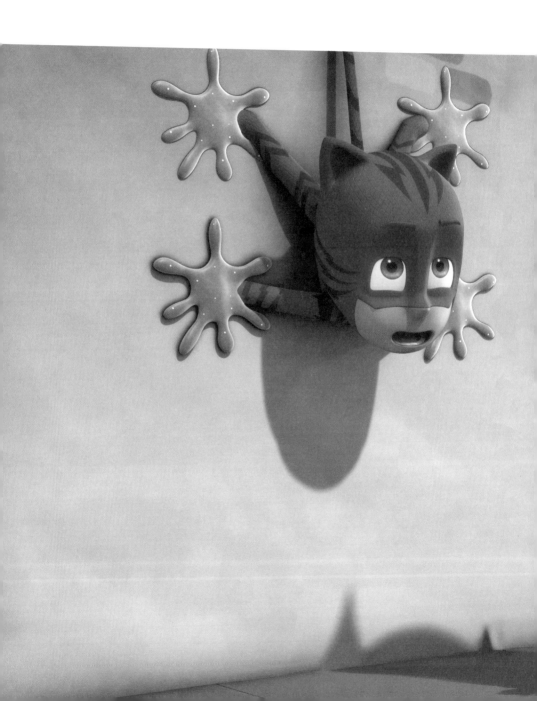

Owlette gets tangled.

"Only I can stop
Night Ninja now!"
Gekko says.

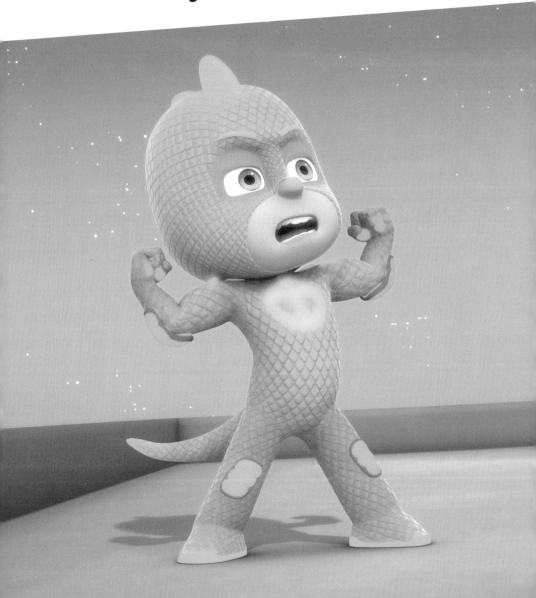

"Super Gekko Muscles!"
Gekko says.
He takes the bus
from Night Ninja.

But Night Ninja steals
the Gekko-Mobile!
Gekko calls for help.

Owlette gets free.

Then she helps Catboy.

Together they help Gekko.

The PJ Masks toss
Night Ninja out of the
Gekko-Mobile.

"You will not beat me next time!"
Night Ninja says.

"When we help each other,
we cannot be beat!"
Gekko says.

The heroes return the bus to school!

Gekko learned that even heroes need help sometimes. Hooray for the PJ Masks!